Mermaids Are Totally... UNREAL

by Adolfo Garza

Beau & Levi

In the unfortunate case that your dreams in life don't come true,
I beg you find happiness with the reality that surrounds you.

Prologue

We live in a society that has provoked our views, opinions, goals and desires by means of the media, advertisements, what's popular on t.v. and whatever else you might fancy out there in cyber space. Many people want what they can't have. They'll imagine something so "perfect" that, at times, they become emotionally numb for trying so hard to attain it; resulting empty-handed in their efforts to do so. Unfortunately, they lose sight on the little things all of us should appreciate and focus on. Great tasting food, the company of our family or friends, great feeling weather, good clean waves graced by soft off-shore winds, seeing in colors and being able to make works of art with them, or even something so subtle as your next breath. This story is intended for those who believe that their happiness is defined by their circumstances. For those who refuse to settle for something they don't really want and can't seem to find what they do. For those who don't know what they want, but are certain that everything in front of them doesn't suffice. So they just keep their eyes on the horizon hoping for something better to come, when nothing ever does. Just a mirage of possibility that keeps them hopeful. Whether it be a great paying career, a position in society, attention from a certain admirer, sublime health or even a sincere true love. At times, it might take double the effort to appreciate reality, as it takes to search for whatever it is you really want, but cannot find.

I hope you enjoy my story, and my art that it took for illustrating it.

Mermaids Are Totally... UNREAL

There was once a boy nobody could understand. He enjoyed playing at the beach, but his taste for life was very bland.

- SCIENCE -
- CIENCIA -

In school, where attention is put to the test, his focus astray; he was so very different from the rest.

Looking outside, dreaming afloat in a far-away galaxy made him go about reality, very callously.

After his studies, this boy would visit a close friend. A retired pirate who lived near the surf. A warm welcome he would always extend.

He cooked the boy food & spoke stories of the sea. Animals he met, even a parrot he found along the way that became his pet. The listening boy felt free with possibility. One night the boy stopped by for some cookies & tall tales. The old pirate began a story with a giant squid and great big killer whales!

The boy had a question he could not let go, of a character halfway through the story and said, "WHOA!" Something he never knew, "A beautiful water-girl creature?" The boy had desire to know.

The pirate said, "She lives around water without any legs, so she lived life happier like a fish instead. Mermaids are their name! If a chap like you ever found one, she'd be the PERFECT dame!"

A sleepless night was all that could follow. For the thought of this girl he was unable to swallow. A mermaid in his fishbowl gave him mindful illusions, resulting in the boy saying, "… Finding a mermaid is my dreams conclusion!"

So he studied so hard and out of control, searching the maps for every water hole. He promised he'd find her by searching the whole globe. Even if it meant him going from North to South Pole.

Finding this mermaid was his ultimate goal.

He left in a hurry, after he packed. Passing the city he grew up in, without looking back. Walking along his towns dark gutter, out came a couple of ducks & an otter. Scared in the dark, he reached for a light in his sack.

"You live around water, and could find one with ease! I'm looking for a mermaid. Can you help me, please?"

But all they could do was laugh at the boy. Thinking he was joking left them tickled with joy.

"Mermaids don't exist, you silly clown," was all they could say...

... as the boy walked away with a frown.

This next spot lit by his lamp, was a place in some woods he would frequent to camp. There the water flowed straight through a dam, where out came a beaver he hoped would get him out of his jam.

"You live around water, and could find one with ease! I'm looking for a mermaid. Can you help me, please?"

All the beaver did was laugh with delight, pointing to a tree he was going to bite.

"Mermaids don't exist, you ridiculous buffoon! You may as well be asking a raccoon! I'm sure there's one to be found in this tree. Once I tear down his house, a good laugh he'll need."

Away walked the boy with the light of a full moon. Hoping to find her in another lagoon.

Now finding himself in a humidly wet area, looking for alligators gave him frightful hysteria. Trying to keep his efforts focused & steady, he ignored the thoughts of their teeth, so deadly. Searching for this monster, he found one at bay; and with a confident voice he yelled at it to say, "You live around water and could find one with ease. FIND ME A MERMAID! ... If you may be so kind to, please."

The laughter was too much for this big, hungry gator. So he said to the boy with a roar even greater, "A comedian like you, I'd have to desist. Have you lost your mind? Mermaids don't exist! If you tell more jokes, I promise not to chomp. You tickle me with humor, in this murky little swamp."

Leaving the river & swamps, to vast oceans galore. A list never-ending of animals to explore.
Asking his question to all that he met. "Have you seen a mermaid? For living my life without
her is making me upset. All you animals live in water & could find one with ease. But this
frustration in asking and you laughing feels like 1000 stinging bees. All I want is one mermaid
to make my life go happy from dull. I'd treat her with all the love & affection I have in my soul.
I've traveled great lengths with the same result overseas. I plead & I'm begging you, can you
help me PLEASE?"

But all the animals were laughing at this poor boy; who's dream of finding his mermaid they were about to destroy. His temper nearly exploded, like a grenade. So he found peace by the ocean, and just thought of his mermaid...

… while strumming a guitar to the sweetest serenade:

"Mermaid, where can you be? I've traveled all over, if only you'd see.
All of your friends sting me with bees,
by me asking them questions and them pointing to trees.
But I hope you're out there looking for me too;
to stop me from feeling like this ocean so blue.
I'm sitting here lonely in this cool sand,
awaiting your beauty to stop my life from being so bland.
If you can hear me, I'm headed where it always snows.
I'll be searching for you in North & South Poles.
Just as I promised, as I'm a man of my word.
I hope you're there waiting, to make my heart fly like a bird."

So just as he promised, he went to the cold. Hoping to find his dream a reality, in North or South Pole. Pitching a tent to find warmth from the frost. There he would sleep and take rest from traveling the distant waters across.

Dreaming of his mermaid in deep sleep, the one he could not even catch to keep.

Not in real life nor in DREAMS could he be so bold, to catch this girl he was wanting more than all of Earth's gold. His confidence began to vanish & dwindle; feeling so small his motivation resulting difficult to rekindle. Standing there with snow up to his knees, feeling his breath starting to wheeze. He felt his desire begin to escape him along with the cold breeze. The sky making colors that started to tease. For the magnetic power he was gazing upon may as well be coming from the most rotten of cheese.

With all the confidence left over he possessed, he searched for a walrus in the midst of distress.

Before giving up, he took one last chance.

"Behold! The Great Walrus!" He saw at a glance.

"May I ask you a question?" The boy said with a sigh, "Please don't think me to be a wise-guy. My question is simple & sincere as can be, so a polite reply to my question is key." To that the walrus replied to say, "Ask your question, and you'll have my attention on this sleepy day, with soft snow to lay on here by this bay."

"You live around water and could find one with ease! I'm looking for a mermaid. Can you help me, please?"

But asking mid-question the walrus took a long nap, and nothing could wake him. Not even a tap.

Walking back to his tent, head hanging low, looking down defeated in the cold, blinding white snow. "What am I doing here alone on this ice?! Even if I found her, would that even suffice? I'm just tired of living this life without spice; spending all my time searching for a girl that may not exist!" This was the only thought that would nag & persist.

"We heard someone here crying inside, and were wondering if there was any help to provide. Is there anything we can do for your grief to subside?" Impassive the boy was from what came from outside. Three little penguins hobbled in puffy by his side, when the boy was wiping away the tears he had cried. Not knowing how to reply because no other animal was willing to comply.

"Thank you for offering Mr. Penguins, that is very kind. But if I tell you what I search for you'd just laugh until you cry. Or say something sarcastic about how much easier it would be to flap your little flippers and flap until you fly. So I think it better I be left alone to sleep until I die."

Thats when the penguins spoke as if answering to a prayer. "No matter how fast these flippers flap, we'll never fly through the air. But why should we care or think life's unfair, when it would be our fault to look at other birds, and then start to compare? You see, flying has been a dream of ours since we hatched from our egg. Now knowing we can never fly, believe us when we tell you we can sympathize. So please, tell us now what you cannot find, before we start to beg."

"A mermaid," said the boy while he began to mourn. "It's been like trying to search for the most beautiful of flowers, but all I can find are simply its thorns." The penguins swam off, promising to help by giving him their word. Then off to find Narwhal the Wise to tell him what they had heard.

It was rumored he got his wisdom through his pointy ivory bone. Surely he'd know what to say to the boy with a hopeless tone. Once the penguins found him swimming in a sea far away, down below; Narwhal the Wise went to be introduced to the boy up on the snow.

Narwhal the Wise listened to every word the boy had said. He wasn't quick to judge, he only noticed the boy was hanging on to his last thread.

"I know it's difficult to appreciate what's around, when the thing you can't find brings you so down. You begin to think what's unfair is LIFE. When the thing you want most is missing, the result only brings you mental strife. But LIFE is the fairest thing of them all! It has air to breath, food to eat and waves to surf that are however tall! Try your best to focus on these things you already have so your mind can surely heal. Now give Narwhal the Wise a great big hug, and lets you & I make a deal. Promise me that you'll focus on the positives of our realities so that positive you'll feel; and I'll tell you a secret that only water creatures know, which you must promise to conceal."

Leaning in, the narwhal tells him...

"Mermaids are TOTALLY... unreal."

The End...

About the Author & Illustrator

Adolfo Garza spent 6 years writing and illustrating the book you hold in your hands. During this time, he traveled the world, using the sights and experiences as inspiration. The story was written on the Big Island of Hawaii, where Adolfo enjoyed surfing and swimming. Among other places, much of the book was illustrated while he was exploring the mountains of the Andes, the vast coastline of South America, the fjords of Patagonia, Tierra del Fuego and the streets of Santiago, Chile.

Connect with Adolfo on Instagram: @dolfo.83